Charles H. Crosse, Marcus Tullius Cicero

M. Tulli Ciceronis Pro P Cornelio Sulla

oratio ad iudices

Charles H. Crosse, Marcus Tullius Cicero

M. Tulli Ciceronis Pro P Cornelio Sulla
oratio ad iudices

ISBN/EAN: 9783337399412

Printed in Europe, USA, Canada, Australia, Japan

Cover: Foto ©Andreas Hilbeck / pixelio.de

More available books at **www.hansebooks.com**

M. TULLI CICERONIS

PRO

P. CORNELIO SULLA

ORATIO AD IUDICES.

LITERALLY TRANSLATED.

By CHARLES H. CROSSE, M.A. & M.I.

(Gonville and Gaius College, Cambridge,)

CAMBRIDGE :—J. HALL AND SON ;

London :—Simpkin, Marshall & Co.; Hamilton,
Adams & Co.

1882.

ARGUMENT.

PUBLIUS CORNELIUS SULLA had been elected consul with Publius Autronius Paetus, for B.C. 65, but was impeached for bribery (*ambitus*), convicted and deprived of his office. T. Manlius Torquatus (son of one of the unsuccessful candidates, who became a consul on Sulla's deprivation) was then, as now B.C. 62., probably in July, the prosecutor. In the trial before us Sulla was impeached under the *lex Plautia de vi* on the charge of being implicated in both of the conspiracies of Cataline. Autronius, who was also accused, endeavoured to retain Cicero for his defence, but Cicero refused to appear for him and even gave evidence against him. But from Sulla Cicero had borrowed 2,000,000 sesterces, and he wished moreover to lay him and his powerful friends under an obligation. Torquatus in his speech for the prosecution had attacked Cicero himself, and endeavoured to damage him with the court by saying that he had taken upon himself the kingly power of acquitting or condemning according to his own will : and calling him the third foreign king that had reigned in Rome, the two former being Numa and Tarquin. This attack seems not to have lessened the friendship between Cicero and Torquatus. Cicero is defending himself almost as much as Sulla. His was the last speech for the defence. Sulla was acquitted.

CICERO'S ORATION

FOR

PUBLIUS SULLA.

CHAPTER I.

1. I SHOULD have been especially glad, O Judges, (to find) that P. Sulla had been able formerly to retain the splendour of his dignified office, and, after the calamity which befel him, to derive some reward from his moderation. But since unfriendly fortune has so brought it to pass, that, even at the time of his greatest honour, he should be upset both by the envy which commonly follows ambition, and by the singular hatred for Autronius, and that, in these sad and deplorable remains of his former fortune, he still should have some (enemies) whose feelings he could not appease even by his own punishment; although from his distresses I receive great vexation in my mind, yet in his other misfortunes I can easily endure that an opportunity should be offered to me, whereby good men should recognise my lenity and merciful disposition, known formerly to all, (but) of late as it were interrupted, (and that) wicked and abandoned citizens, defeated and vanquished, should confess that when the republic was in danger I was energetic and brave, now that it is saved I am lenient and merciful.

2. And since L. Torquatus, my intimate and friend, O judges, has thought that if in his accusation he had violated our friendship and intimacy, he might detract somewhat from the

A

authority of my defence, I will unite a defence, of my own
duty with the warding off danger *from my client (hujus)*. That
sort of speech indeed I would not employ, O Judges, at this
time, if my own interest alone were concerned; for in many
places the opportunity has been given me and often will be
given of speaking of my own credit : but as he, (has
thought) that the more he detracted from my authority the
more he would be likely to diminish my client's means of
protection, so I think this, that if I shall recommend to you
the principles of my conduct and my perseverance in this duty
and defence, I shall recommend also the cause of P. Sulla.

3.   And in the first place, L. Torquatus, I ask this from
you why you should separate me from the other very illustrious
men and leaders of this city in the matter of this duty and in
the right of defence ? For what is the reason why the act of
Q. Hortensius, a most illustrious and most accomplished man,
is not blamed by you, (whereas) mine is blamed ? For if a
plan of firing the city, of extinguishing the empire, of destroy-
ing the state was entertained by P. Sulla, ought not those
things to cause greater indignation and greater hatred in me
than in Q. Hortensius, in short, ought not my opinion to be
more strict as to who should be assisted in these causes, who
should be opposed, who defended, who abandoned ? "Certainly,"
he says, "for you have investigated, you have laid open the
conspiracy."

CHAPTER II.

4.   AND when he says this, he does not perceive that he
who laid it open took care of this, that all should see, that which
before had been hidden. Wherefore that conspiracy, if it has
been laid open by me, is just as evident to Hortensius as to
me. And when you see that he, a man endowed with such
rank, authority, virtue, wisdom, has not hesitated to defend

this innocent P. Sulla, I ask why the access to the cause which was open to Hortensius ought to be closed against me. I ask this also, if you think that I ought to be blamed who defend him, what I pray do you think of these most exalted and most illustrious citizens, by whose zeal and dignity you perceive that this trial is attended, this cause is adorned, my client's (*hujus*) innocence is defended? For that is not the only method of defence which consists in making a speech:. all who are present, who are anxious (about him) who wish him safe, defend (him) as far as their opportunity and authority allow.

5. Ought I indeed to be unwilling to appear on these benches on which I see these ornaments and lights of the republic, I who have mounted into their rank and into this most exalted position of dignity and honour by my own many and great labours and dangers? And that you may understand, Torquatus, whom you are accusing, if perchance this offends you, that I, who in this kind of enquiry have defended no-one, do not abandon P. Sulla, call to mind also the other men whom you see present in this man's favour: you will understand that concerning this man and concerning others my opinion and theirs has been one and the same.

6. Who of us countenanced Varguntius? No one, not even this Hortensius, he especially who alone had defended him formerly on a charge of corruption. For he did not think that he was connected with him by any tie of duty, when he, by the commission of so great wickedness, had broken asunder the tie of all duties whatever. Who of us thought Servius Sulla, who thought Publius, who thought M. Læca, who thought C. Cornelius fit to be defended? Who of these countenanced them? No-one. Why so? Because in other causes good men think that they ought not to desert even the guilty, if they are intimate friends: but in this prosecution there is not only the fault of lightmindedness, but also a certain infection of wickedness, if you should defend him whom you suspect to be involved in (planning) the parricide of his country.

7. What? In the case of Autronius, did not his companions, did not his colleagues, did not his former friends, in abundance of whom he formally abounded, did not all these, who are the chief men in the republic, desert him? Yea many of them even damaged him by their evidence. They had come to the conclusion that it was so great an offence that it not only ought not to be concealed by them, but even to be revealed and elucidated.

CHAPTER III.

WHEREFORE what reason is there why you should wonder, if you see me giving countenance in this cause, with those same men with whom you know that I joined in discountenancing the other causes? Unless indeed you wish me alone beyond other men to be considered fierce, harsh, inhuman, endowed with extraordinary barbarity and cruelty.

8. If on account of my exploits you fix this character on me throughout my whole life, Torquatus, you are greatly mistaken. Nature willed me to be merciful, my country (made me) severe, but neither my country nor nature has willed me to be cruel. Lastly, that same vehement and fierce character which at that time the occasion and the republic imposed upon me, my inclination and nature itself has now taken away. For the former required severity for a short time, the latter during my whole life has required clemency and lenity.

9. Wherefore there is no reason why you should separate me from so numerous a company of most honourable men : duty is plain, and the cause of all good men is the same. There will be no reason why you should wonder hereafter, if you shall see me on the same side on which you observe these men. For there is no side in the republic (which is) my peculiar (property) : the time for acting did belong more peculiarly to me than to others, but that cause for indignation and fear and

danger was a common one: for I could not at that time have been the first (to provide) for the safety (of the state), if others had been unwilling to be (my) companions. Wherefore it is necessary that that which was peculiar to me as consul above others, should be common to me now as a private person with the rest. Nor do I say this for the sake of causing them to participate in my unpopularity, but (for the sake) of causing them to share in my praise: I give a share of my burden to no one, but (a share) of my glory to all good men.

10. "You gave testimony against Autronius," says he, "you are defending Sulla." This entirely tends to prove, O judges, that if I am inconstant and fickle-minded, it will not be fitting that credit should be paid to my testimony, nor authority to my defence: but if there is in me a regard for the republic, a scrupulous consideration for my private duty, a desire to retain the good will of good men, then (there is) nothing (which) an accuser ought to say less than that Sulla is defended by me, and that Autronius was injured by my testimony. For I seem now to bring (with me) not only zeal in defending causes, but also somewhat of opinion and authority: which I shall use moderately, O judges, and I would not have used at all, if he had not compelled me.

CHAPTER IV.

11. Two conspiracies are put forward by you, O Torquatus; one which is said to have been formed when Lepidus and Volcatius were consuls, your own father being consul elect; the other that which (was formed) when I was consul: in both of these you say Sulla was implicated. You know that I was not acquainted with the counsels of your father, a most brave man, and a most excellent consul: you know,

since, between you and me there was the greatest intimacy, yet that I was not privy to what happened or what was said : I suppose because I was not yet thoroughly versed in the affairs of the state, because I had not yet arrived at the goal of honour proposed to myself, because ambition and forensic labour was separating me from all deliberations of that kind.

12. Who then was present at your counsels? All these men whom you see to be giving countenance to this man (Sulla), and especially Q. Hortensius : who, both because of his honour and worth, and excellent disposition towards the republic, and because of his excessive intimacy with an excessive love towards your father, was moved both by the common (dangers) and by the special perils of your father. Therefore the charge of (being implicated in) that conspiracy was warded off by that man who was present at, who was cognizant of, who was a sharer in all your designs and fears : whose speech, most elegant and most eloquent as it was in repelling this accusation, yet had in it no less authority than ability. Of that conspiracy therefore, which is said to have been formed against you, reported to you, revealed by you, I was not able to be a witness : I not only found out nothing in my own mind, but scarcely did any report of that suspicion reach to my ears.

13. Those who were in your counsel, who were cognizant with you of these things, who themselves were thought at that time to be mixed up in the danger, who did not countenance Autronius, who gave important evidence against him, (these) are defending my client (Sulla), are countenancing him, (and) in this (time of) his danger they declare that they were deterred from countenancing the others, not by the charge of conspiracy, but by the guilt of the men. But the time of my consulship and the charge of the greatest conspiracy shall be defended by me. And this partition (of the cause) between us has not been made at random, O judges, nor rashly, but since we saw that we were employed as ad-

vocates in those charges in which we might have been witnesses, each of us thought that (part of the case) ought to be undertaken by him, concerning which he himself had been able to acquire some knowledge and to form an opinion.

CHAPTER V.

14. AND since you have attentively listened to Hortensius concerning the charges of the former conspiracy, with reference to this conspiracy, which was formed when I was consul, attend first to this statement.

When I was consul, I heard many things concerning the extreme perils of the republic, I made enquiries, I gained much information : with reference to Sulla no messenger, no information, no letters, no suspicion ever reached me. Perhaps this assertion ought to have great weight, (as being the assertion) of that man who, as consul, had investigated the plots against the republic with wisdom, had revealed them with sincerity, had punished them with greatness of mind, (especially) when he says that he heard nothing against P. Sulla, never entertained any suspicion. But I do not yet employ this assertion for defending him : I shall use it rather to clear myself, that Torquatus may cease to wonder that I, who did not countenance Autronius, am defending Sulla.

15. For what was the cause of Autronius ? What is that of Sulla ? The former (Autronius), attempted to get rid of and disturb a prosecution for bribery in the first place by raising a tumult of gladiators and fugitive slaves, and, in the second place, as we all saw, by stoning (people) and by (collecting) a mob : Sulla, if his own modesty and dignity could not avail him, sought no (other) assistance. The former (Autronius), when convicted so behaved himself, not only in

his plans and conversations, but even in look and countenance, as to appear an enemy to the most honourable orders, hostile to all good men, an enemy to his country : the latter, (Sulla), considered himself so broken and bowed down by that calamity, that he thought that nothing of his former dignity remained to him, except what he had retained by moderation.

16. Moreover in this conspiracy, what so united as Autronius (*ille*) with Cataline, with Lentulus ? What partnership (was there ever) between any men for good purposes, so intimate as his with them (for purposes) of wickedness, lust, audacity ? What crime did not Lentulus plot with Autronius ? What wickedness did Cataline commit without him ? While in the meantime Sulla not only did not seek (the concealment of) night and solitude with those same men, but was not even mixed up with them in ordinary conversation or conference.

17. The Allobroges, the truest informers on most important matters, accused him, the letters and messengers of many men accused him : Meanwhile no one accused Sulla, no one mentioned his name. Lastly, when Cataline had been driven out or sent out now from the city, Autronius (*ille*) sent (him) arms, trumpets, bugles, fasces, standards, Autronius (*ille*) left within (the city), expected out of it, checked by the punishment of Lentulus, turned himself sometimes to (feelings of fear), never to discretion : Sulla (*hic*), on the other hand, was so quiet, that during all that time he was at Naples, where it is not supposed that there were (any) men implicated in this suspicion, and the place itself is not so calculated to inflame the feelings of those distressed, as to console them.

CHAPTER VI.

18. On account therefore of this so great dissimilarity between the men and the causes, I behaved in a different manner to both. For Autronius came to me and kept

on coming often, with many tears beseeching me to defend him, and used to remind me that he had been my school fellow in my boyhood, my intimate friend in my youth, my colleague in the quæstorship : he used to bring forward many kindnesses of mine towards him, some also of his own towards me. By which circumstances, O judges, I was so swayed in mind and moved, that I banished from my memory all the plots which he had laid against me myself, that I forgot that lately C. Cornelius had been sent by him to kill me in my own house, in sight of my wife and children.

19. And if he had meditated these things against me alone, of such softness and lenity of disposition am I, that never indeed could I have resisted his tears and prayers ; but when (thoughts) of my country, of your danger, of this city, of those shrines and temples, of infant children, of matrons and virgins came into my mind, and when those hostile and deadly torches, and the whole conflagration of the entire city, when the weapons, the slaughter and blood of the citizens, when the ashes of my country began to present themselves before my eyes and to excite my mind by the recollection (of them), then at last I resisted him, and not only (did I resist) that enemy and parricide himself, but also his relations, the Marcelli, father and son, of whom the one possessed with me the weight of a parent, the other the affection of a son : and I thought that I could not, without the greatest wickedness, defend in their companion the same crime which I had punished in others, (especially) when I knew (that he was guilty of it).

20. And I the same person could not endure (to see) P. Sulla (coming as) a suppliant, nor to behold those same Marcelli weeping at his danger, nor could I resist the en-treaties of this M. Messula here, a man with whom I am very intimate : for neither was the cause opposed to nature, nor was the man or the fact repugnant to my (feeling of) pity.

His name had never been (mentioned) there was no trace
(of him in the conspiracy), no charge, no information, no
suspicion against him. I undertook his cause, O Torquatus,
I undertook it, and I did so willingly, in order that while
good men, as I hope, had always thought me firm, not even
bad men should call me cruel.

CHAPTER VII.

21. This Torquatus here says that he, O judges, cannot
endure my kingly power. What kingly power, I pray, O
Torquatus? (That) of my consulship, I suppose (you mean):
in which I did not command at all, and on the contrary
obeyed the conscript fathers and all good men: in which
magistracy kingly power was not established by me forsooth,
but put down. Or do you say that then, in (the exercise of)
so great authority and power, I was not a king, but now,
(when only) a private person, I possess kingly power? On
what grounds, I pray (do you say so)? Because those against
whom you gave testimony, says he, have been condemned,
the man whom you are defending hopes that he shall be
acquitted. Here I make you this reply concerning my
evidence: if I gave false evidence, you also gave evidence
against the same persons: but (if I gave) true evidence, (then
I say) that this does not constitute kingly power, (namely)
to convince (the judges), when on oath you gave true evidence.

22. Concerning my clients hope, this only I say, that P.
Sulla expects no assistance from me, no influence, nothing in
short except sincerity of defence. "But unless you," says he,
"had undertaken his cause, he would never have resisted me,
"but would have with his cause unheard fled." If now I should
grant you this, that Q. Hortensius, a man of such importance, if,

that these so great men, do not rely on their own judgment but on mine: if I should grant this to you, which cannot be credited, that unless I had countenanced this man (Sulla) these would not countenance him, which I pray is the king, he whom innocent men cannot resist, or he who does not abandon men in misfortune ? But here also, a thing which was least necessary for you, you chose to be facetious, when you called me Tarquin and Numa, and said that I was the third foreign king (of Rome). I pass over now any enquiry, as to the word king, this I enquire, why you called me a foreigner. For if I am such, it is not so much to be wondered at that I am a king, since, as you say, even foreigners have been kings at Rome, as that a foreigner should have been a consul at Rome.

23. "I mean this," says he, "that you are from a municipal town." I confess it, and I add also (that I come) from that municipal town, whence repeatedly already safety to this city and empire has proceeded. But I should much like to know from you why those who come from municipal towns appear to you to be foreigners. No one ever made that objection to M. Cato the elder, though he had many enemies; no one (made it) to Ti. Coruncanius, no one (made it) to M. Curius, no one (made it) to this celebrated C. Marius of ours, though many envied him. Indeed I am greatly delighted that I am such a man, on whom you, when you, desired it, were able to cast no reproach, which did not apply to the greatest part of the citizens.

CHAPTER VIII.

BUT yet, on the great pretext of our intimacy, I think you ought to be reminded (of this) again and again. All cannot be patricians: if you seek (to know) the truth, they

do not even care (to be) : nor do those of your own age think
that on that account you ought to have precedence.

24. And if to you we seem to be foreigners, whose
name and honour already has become familiar both to this
city and to the talk and conversation of men, how necessary
will it be for those competitors of yours to seem to be
foreigners, who, chosen now from all Italy, are contending
with you for honour and every dignity : but do you beware
of calling anyone of these a foreigner, lest you should be overwhelmed by the votes of the foreigners. For if they bring
their activity and perseverance (into play), believe me, they
will shake out of you that wordy boasting, and will often rouse
you from sleep, and will not suffer themselves to be surpassed
by you in honour, unless they are excelled in virtue.

25. But if, O judges, it is fitting for me and you to be
thought foreigners, by other patricians, yet by Torquatus nothing
ought to be said about this defeat. For he himself is on his
mothers' side (a citizen) of a municipal (town), of a most honourable and noble family, but nevertheless an Asculanian. Either
therefore let him show that the Picentians alone are not
foreigners, or let him rejoice that I do not put my family
before his. Wherefore do not you hereafter call me a
foreigner, lest you should be more sternly refuted, nor a
king lest you be laughed at. Unless perchance it seems to
you to be the part of a king so to live, as not only not to be a
slave to any man, but not even to any passion, to despise all
lusts, to covet neither gold, nor silver, nor other things,
to form opinions in the senate freely, to consult more for the
interest of the people than for their inclination, to yield to
no-one, to oppose many. If you think this to be kingly,
I confess that I am a king : but if my power, if my sway,
if in short any arrogant or proud expression of mine moves
you, why do you not allege that, rather than the odium and
contumely of a mere word ?

CHAPTER IX.

26. IF, so many services having been done by me to the republic, I were to ask no other reward for myself from the Senate and people of Rome than honourable ease, who would not grant it? (If I were to ask that) they should keep for themselves (all) honours, commands, provinces, triumphs, and (all) other insignia of eminent renown : (if only) it were allowed to me to enjoy with tranquil and quiet mind a sight of that city which I had saved—(who would not grant it?) What? if I do not ask this: (what) if that former industry of mine, my anxiety, my services, my exertions, my vigilance is at the command of my friends, is ready for all : if neither my friends in the forum seek in vain for my zeal, nor the republic in the senate house : if, not only the exemption earned by my (previous) achievements, but the excuse either of honour (already gained) or of age, does not save me from toil : if my good-will, my industry, my house, my disposition, my ears are open to all : if no time is left me to remember and think over those things indeed which I have done for the safety of all, nevertheless shall this be called kingly power, (when) no one can be found who would wish to act as my substitute in it?

27. The suspicion of (aiming at) kingly power is far removed from me. If you ask who have endeavoured at Rome to seize on kingly power, that you may not unfold the records of the (public) annals, you may find them among the images in your house. For my achievements, I suppose, have too much elated me, and have brought to me I know not how much pride. Concerning which things, so illustrious, so immortal, O judges, I can say this, that I, who from the most extreme dangers have saved this city, and the lives of all the citizens, shall have gained sufficient reward, if, out of this so great service towards all men, no danger shall have arisen to myself.

28. For I remember in what state I have done such great exploits, I understand in what city I am living. The forum is full of those men, whom I have driven away from your necks, O judges, (but) have not removed from my own. Unless indeed you think that they were few in number who were able to attempt or to hope that they might destroy so vast an empine. I was able to take away their torches from their hands, and to wrest away their swords, as I did, but their wicked and impious inclinations I was able neither to cure nor to eradicate. Wherefore I am not ignorant in how great danger I am living among so vast a multitude of wicked men, since I see that by me alone an eternal war has been undertaken against all wicked men.

CHAPTER X.

29. BUT if perchance you envy those my means of protection, and if they seem to you to be of a kingly nature —(namely the fact) that all good men of all classes and ranks join their own safety with mine, (it behoves you) to console yourself (with the fact) that the minds of all wicked men are especially hostile and opposed to me alone : and these hate me, not alone on this account, because I repressed their impious attempts and wicked fury, but on this account even more, because they think that they are able to attempt nothing now of the same sort, while I am alive.

30. But indeed why should I wonder, if anything is said wickedly about me by wicked men, when L. Torquatus himself after having in the first place laid such foundations of his youth, and having set before himself such hope of the most honourable dignity, and in the second place being the son of L. Torquatus, a most brave consul, a most virtuous senator, and always a most excellent citizen—sometimes is

carried away by impetuosity of language ? For when he had spoken in suppressed voice of the wickedness of P. Lentulus, and of the audacity of all the conspirators, so that you only, who approve of those things, could thoroughly hear (what he was saying), spoke in a loud and querulous voice of the punishment of P. Lentulus and of the prison.

31. In which, first of all, this was absurd, that when he wished to gain your approval of those things which he had said inconsiderately, but did not wish those to hear them, who were standing around the tribunal, he did not perceive that you also who did not approve would hear those things which he was speaking loudly so that those should hear for whom he was prostituting himself : and in the second place another defect of an orator (is) not to see what each cause requires. For nothing is so unfavourable for him who is accusing another of conspiracy, as to appear to grieve for the punishment and death of conspirators. When that tribune of the people does. it, who seems to be the only one of them left to bewail the conspirators, it is a matter of wonder to no one : for it is difficult to be silent when you are grieving : but I greatly wonder at you, if you do anything of that sort, not only (because you are) such a young man, but (because you do this) in that cause in which you wish yourself to be a punisher of conspiracy.

32. But I blame this most, that you, endowed with such ability and prudence, do not maintain the cause of the republic, (but are one) who believes. that those actions are not approved of by the Roman people, which, when I was consul, all good men did for the common safety.

CHAPTER XI.

Do you believe that anyone of those who are present, into whose favour you were seeking to insinuate yourself

against their own will, was either so wicked as to wish all
these things to perish, or so miserable as to wish to perish
himself, and to have nothing which he should wish to be
preserved ? Or indeed does anyone blame that most illustrious
man of your family and name, who deprived his own son
of life that he might strengthen his power over others ? do
you (then) blame the republic, which destroyed domestic
enemies lest it should itself be destroyed by them ?

33.   Therefore notice, O Torquatus, how I withdraw
from the responsibility of my consulship. With my loudest
voice, so that all may be able to hear, I speak and always
will speak ; be present all (of you) with (your) minds, who
are present with (your) bodies, in whose numerous attendance
I greatly rejoice : prick up your minds and your ears and
listen to me speaking on unpopular topics, as he thinks ! I,
as consul, when an army of abandoned citizens, excited by
clandestine wickedness, had prepared a most cruel and miserable destruction for (my) country, when, for the fall and
ruin of the republic, Cataline (had been appointed leader) in
the camp, and Lentulus had been appointed leader among
these temples and houses, by my plans, by my labours, at the
risk of my own life, without a tumult, without a levy, without
arms, without an army, having seized five men and executed
them, I freed the city from conflagration, the citizens from
massacre, Italy from devastation, the republic from destruction : I ransomed the life of all the citizens, the security of
the whole world, this city in short, the home of us all
the citadel of foreign kings and nations, the light of nations,
the abode of empire, by the punishment of five mad and
abandoned men.

34.   Or did you think that I would not say this unsworn
in a court of justice, which, when on oath, I had said in a
most numerous assembly ?

CHAPTER XII.

AND this also I will add, lest perchance any wicked man should begin suddenly to become attached to you, O Torquatus, or to hope anything from you, and, that all may thoroughly hear it, I will say it with a very loud voice : of all these things, which I, in my consulship, for the safety of the republic, undertook and carried on, that very L. Torquatus, when he was my comrade in the consulship, and also had been in the prætorship, stood forth as my adviser, assistant and partner, when he was (also) the chief, and the leader and the standard-bearer of the (Roman) youth: and his father, a man most devoted to his country, (a man) of the greatest courage, of the most consummate ability, and of conspicuous firmness, though he was ill, yet was present at all those actions : he never departed from me : by his zeal, advice, authority, he alone assisted me very much, since he overcame the infirmity of his body by the vigour of his mind.

35. Do not you see how I deliver you from the sudden favour of the wicked and reconcile you to all good men ? who both love you and cherish you and will cherish you always, nor if perchance you shall have withdrawn from me, on that account will they suffer you to abandon them and the republic and your own dignity.

But now I return to the cause, and I call you to bear witness to this, O judges ; that a certain necessity has been imposed on me by him of speaking of myself so much. For if Torquatus had accused Sulla alone, I indeed at this time should have done nothing else but defend him who had been accused, but when he, in his whole speech, had inveighed against me, and when as I said at the beginning he had tried to deprive my defence of its authority, even if my indignation had not compelled me to answer, yet the cause itself would have required this speech from me.

CHAPTER XIII.

36. You say that Sulla was named by Allobroges. Who denies it? But read the indictment and see how he was named. They said that L. Cassius asserted that, together with others, Autronius acted with him. I ask, did Cassius say that Sulla (acted with him)? Never. They say that they themselves enquired of Cassius what opinions Sulla held. Observe the diligence of the Gauls: who did not know the (previous) life and character of the man and had only heard that they were in the same calamity, (but) asked whether they were of the same inclination? What then as to Cassius? If he had answered that Sulla did hold the same sentiments and acted with him, yet it would not seem to me that this ought to be made a matter of accusation against him. Why so? Because, (in the case of one) who was instigating the barbarians to war, it was no business of his to weaken their suspicion, and to acquit those men of whom they seemed to entertain some suspicions.

37. But he did not reply however that Sulla acted with him. Moreover, it would have been absurd, when he had named others of his own accord, to make no mention of Sulla until admonished and asked: unless perchance it is likely that the name of P. Sulla did not come into the memory of Cassius. If the high rank of the man, if his unfortunate condition, if the relics of his former dignity had not been so notorious, yet the mention of Autronius must have brought back the recollection of Sulla; moreover, as I think, when Cassius was enumerating the authority of the chiefs of the conspiracy for the purpose of stirring up the minds of the Allobroges, and when he knew that foreign nations are especially moved by high rank, he would not have named Autronius before Sulla.

38. Now indeed this can by no means be proved, that the Gauls, when Autronius was named, thought that on

account of the similarity of their misfortune they ought to enquire anything about Sulla, (yet that), if he (Sulla) was implicated in the same wickedness, not even when he (Cassius) had mentioned Autronius, could (the name of Sulla) occur to the mind of Cassius. But however, what did Cassius answer about Sulla? That he knew nothing for certain. "He does not acquit him," says (Torquatus). I have said before : not even if he had accused him indeed then at length, when he had beed interrogated, does that seem to me a (fair) matter of accusation (against Sulla).

39. But I think that in investigations and examinations not this should be enquired, whether anyone is exculpated, but whether he is inculpated. For when Cassius says that he does not know, does he support Sulla, or clearly prove that he does not know? "He supports him with the Gauls." Why so? That they may not indict him? What? if he had thought that there was no danger, lest they should ever indict him, would he himself have made that confession about himself? "He did not know forsooth." I suppose that Cassius was kept in the dark about Sulla only : for about others he had certain knowledge : for it is clearly proved that most (of the conspiracy) was hatched at his house. He who was unwilling to deny that Sulla was in that number (of conspirators), but did not dare to say what was false, said that he did not know. And this is clear, that when he, who knew (the truth) about all, said that he did not know about Sulla, the weight of this denial is the same, as if he had said that he knew that he (Sulla) had nothing to do with the conspiracy. For when anyone's knowledge of all (the conspirators) is clearly proved to have existed, his ignorance of anyone ought to be considered an acquittal. But I am not now enquiring whether Cassius acquits Sulla : this is quite sufficient for me, that there is nothing in the indictment against Sulla.

CHAPTER XIV.

40. BEING cut off from this (part of his) accusation Torquatus again rushes upon me and accuses me: he says that I have made an entry in the public registers different to what was (really) spoken. O immortal gods!—for I will pay you that tribute which is yours, nor can I grant so much to my own ability, as (to think) that I managed, of my own power, affairs so many, so important, so various, so sudden, during that most turbulent tempest of the republic,— you in truth then inflamed my mind with the desire of saving my country: you turned me from all other thoughts to the one (idea of the) safety of the republic: you in short in so great darkness of error and ignorance held a most bright light before my mind.

41. I saw this, O judges, that unless, while the memory of the senate was fresh, I bore evidence to the authority of this information by public records, it would come to pass that hereafter not Torquatus nor any one like Torquatus,— for that has greatly deceived me,—but that some one, wrecked of his patrimony, an enemy of tranquility, a foe to (all) good men, should say that these things had been otherwise stated in the indictment, in order that more easily, when some gale had been stirred up against every good man, he might be able, amid the misfortunes of the republic, to find some harbour for his own misfortunes. Therefore, having introduced into the senate informers, I appointed senators to write down all the statements of the informers, the questions and the answers.

42. But what men (were they)! not only (men) of the highest virtue and good faith, of which sort there was in the senate the greatest plenty, but also (men) whom I knew, from their memory, their knowledge, their rapidity of writing, could most easily follow everything that was said: (viz.)

C. Cosconius, who then was prætor, M. Messala who then was a candidate for the prætorship, P. Nigidius, App. Claudius. I believe there is no one who thinks that these men were deficient either in the good faith or talent (necessary) to give an accurate report.

CHAPTER XV.

WHAT next? What did I do? Since I knew that thus the information would be entered in the public records, but yet that those records would be kept in private custody, according to the custom of our ancestors, I did not conceal (the information), I did not keep it at home, but I ordered it immediately to be copied by all the copyists, to be distributed everywhere, and to be published and made known to the Roman people. I distributed it all over Italy, I sent it into all the provinces, I wished no one to be ignorant of that information from which safety was procured for all.

43. Therefore I say, that there is no spot in the world where the name of the Roman people is (known) where this written information has not arrived. And in this so sudden and brief and disturbed opportunity, I took many precautions by divine providence, as I have said, not of my own accord : (taking the precaution) in the first place, that no one should be able to recollect of the danger to the republic or to any individual only as much as he pleased : and in the second place that no one could ever find fault with that information, or accuse (us) of having rashly credited it : and lastly, that no one should seek (to learn) anything now from me, or anything from my notes, lest either my forgetfulness or memory should seem too great, lest in short either my negligence should be thought discreditable, or my diligence cruel.

44. But yet from you, Torquatus, I ask, since your enemy was mentioned in the information, and a crowded senate and the fresh memory (of all) is a witness, and my clerks would have communicated the information to you, my intimate friend and companion, if you had wished for it, even before they had copied it, when you saw that they had copied it incorrectly, why were you silent, why did you permit it? why did you not complain to me or to some friend of mine? or, since you so easily inveigh against your friends, (why did you not) expostulate passionately or earnestly? Do you, when your voice was never heard, when, though the information was read, copied, published, (yet) you were quiet, you were silent, (do you I say) suddenly put forth so important a statement, and bring yourself into such a position, that before you convict me of having tampered with the information, you must confess that you are convicted of the grossest negligence, on your own information?

CHAPTER XVI.

45. WAS the safety of anyone of such consequence to me, that I should neglect my own? (or that) I should contaminate by any lie, the truth which had been laid open by me? in short that I would assist anyone, by whom I thought that so cruel a plot had been laid against the republic, and especially when I was consul? But if now I had forgotten my own strictness and firmness, was I so mad, that, when letters have been devised for the sake of posterity, in order that they may be a protection against forgetfulness, I should think that the fresh memory of the whole senate could be overcome by my journal?

46. I am bearing with you, O Torquatus, now for a long time, I am bearing with you, and sometimes I myself call

back and check my mind provoked to chastise your speech : I make allowance somewhat for your irascibility, I grant (something) to your youth, I yield to our friendship, I have a regard for your father. But unless you yourself place some restraint on yourself, you will compel me to forget our friendship (in order) to have regard for my own dignity. No one ever touched me with the slightest suspicion, which I have not put down and shattered. But I wish you to give credit to me in this : I am not wont to answer those most willingly, whom I think I can most easily overcome.

47. Do you, since you are by no means ignorant of my manner of speaking, forbear to abuse this new lenity of mine ; forbear to think that the strings of my eloquence are cut out, because they are hidden ; forbear to think that it has been altogether lost by me, if it has been at all relaxed and withdrawn from you. In the first place (*quum*) these excuses for your injurious conduct avail with me, your angry temper, your age, our friendship, in the second place (*tum*) I do not yet consider you to have sufficient power that I ought to strive and argue with you. But if you were more strong through experience and age, I should be the same as I am wont (to be) when I have been provoked ; at present I shall so deal with you that I shall seem rather to have received an injury than to have returned a favour.

CHAPTER XVII.

48. Nor indeed can I understand why you are angry with me. If it is because I am defending a man whom you are accusing, why should not I be angry with you for accusing a man whom I am defending ? "I am accusing my "enemy," you say. "And I am defending my friend," (I reply). "But you ought not to defend anyone on "a trial for conspiracy "

(you say). Nay rather no-one ought more readily (to defend) him of whom he has never suspected anything, than he who has entertained many suspicions about others. "Why did you give testimony against others?" Because I was compelled. "Why were they convicted?" Because (my evidence) was believed. "It is a kingly conduct to speak against whomsoever "you please and to defend whomsoever you please." Nay rather it is slavish 'conduct not to speak against whomsoever you please and not to defend whom you please. And if you begin to consider whether it was more necessary for me to do this or you to do that, you will perceive that you could more honourably place a limit to your enmities than I could to my humanity.

49. But in truth when the greatest honour of your family was at stake, that is (to say) the consulship of your father, that very wise man your father was not angry with his most intimate friends, when they both defended and praised Sulla. He was aware that this principle has been handed down to us from our ancestors, that we should not be hindered by our friendship for anyone from warding off dangers (from others). But that contest was very far from being similar to this trial: at that time, if P. Sulla could be crushed, the the consulship would be procured for your father (*vobis*), as it was procured : that was a contest for honour : you were crying out that you were seeking to recover what had been snatched away from you, in order that, having been defeated in the Campus Martius, you might be successful in the forum : at that time those who were contending against you for his (Sulla's) safety, your greatest friends, with whom you were not angry (on that account), were trying to snatch away the consulship from you, were resisting your (acquisition of) honour; and they did this without violating your friendship, their duty remaining intact, according to ancient precedent and the principle of every good man.

CHAPTER XVIII.

50. But what honours of yours am I opposing; or what dignity of yours am I fighting against? What is there which you now can seek from this (procceding)? Honour (has been conferred) on your father, the insignia of honour have descended to you. You, adorned with his spoils, come to lacerate him whom you have slain : I am defending and protecting him who is lying (helpless) and stripped (of his armour). And hereupon you both blame me, because I defend him, and are angry. But I not only am not angry with you, but I do not even find fault with your proceeding. For I suppose that you have laid down for yourself what you think you ought to do, and that you have been able to be a sufficiently capable judge of your duty.

51. "But" (perhaps you say) "the son of C. Cornelius "accuses him, and that ought to have the same weight as if "the father had given information." O wise father Cornelius, who relinquished all the reward which is wont to be (given) for an information, and whatever disgrace (there is) in a confession, that he has incurred through the accusation of his son ! But what is it, I pray, which Cornelius gives information of through that boy ? If something of old standing, unknown to me, but communicated to Hortensius, let Hortensius answer : but if, as you say, (it has reference to) that attempt of Autronius and Cataline, when, in the Campus Martius, at the consular comitia which were held by me, they intended to commit a massacre : (then I answer) we saw Autronius at that time in the Campus Martius; but why did I say *we* saw (*him*) ? I myself saw him : for you at that time, O judges, had no anxiety, no suspicions, I, protected by a firm guard of friends, at that time checked the forces and attempt of Cataline and Autronius.

52. Is there then anyone who says that at that time

D

Sulla aspired (to come) into the Campus Martius? And yet, if at that time he had united himself with Cataline in a bond of wickedness, why did he withdraw from him? Why was he not with Autronius? why in a similar case are not similar proofs of criminality found? But since Cornelius himself even now hesitates about giving information, as you say, and forms to this the shadowy information of his son, what I pray does he say about that night, when, on an intimation given him by Cataline, he came into the Scythe-maker's street, (*inter falcarios*), to (the house of) M. Læca, on that night which followed *the sixth of November*, when I was consul? that night which of all the periods of the conspiracy was the most terrible and most bitter. Then the day of Cataline's leaving (the city), then the terms of remaining for the rest, then the arrangement of slaughter and conflagration throughout the city was settled: then your father, O Cornelius, a fact which at length afterwards he confessed, demanded for himself that employment as his duty, that he should go at early dawn to salute me as consul, and having been admitted both in accordance with my custom and by the privilege of frendship he should kill me in my bed.

CHAPTER XIX.

53. At this time, when the conspiracy was burning very strongly, when · Cataline was starting for the army, (and) Lentulus was being left in the city, (when) Cassius was being set over the conflagrations, Cethegus over the massacre, when it was being assigned to Autronius to occupy Etruria, when all things were being arranged, settled, prepared, where was Sulla, O Cornelius? Was he at Rome? Nay rather, he was far away. Was he in those districts to which Cataline was betaking himself? (He was) even much further away: was he in the Camertine district, or in the Picenian, or in the Gallic, into

which regions a certain disease as it were of that frenzy had chiefly spread? nothing (is) less (near) to the truth. For he was, as I have already previously stated, at Naples : he was in that part of Italy which was most free from that suspicion.

54. What then does he state in his information, or what does either Cornelius himself allege, or you, who bring these messages from him? (He alleges) "that gladiators were bought under some pretence of Faustus for slaughter and tumult." Precisely so : the gladiators are mentioned, whom we see by his fathers will he was bound to provide.—(But you will say) "a (whole) household (of slaves) was carried off, and "if this had been left alone, another household might have "discharged the duty of Faustus."—I wish indeed this same household could satisfy, not only the envy of those unfavourable, but the expectation of those favourable!—"He hurried on desperately, when the time for the exhibition was far off."—As if indeed the time for giving the exhibition was not drawing very near.—"The household was obtained without Faustus having any idea of it, when he neither knew of it, nor wished it."

55. But there are letters of Faustus's, in which he with entreaties makes request of P. Sulla to buy gladiators; and to buy these very ones, nor (were these letters) sent only to Sulla, but to L. Cæsar, Q. Pompeius, C. Memmius, by whose advice the whole business was carried on.—"But he was set over the troop."—Now if in obtaining the troop there is no suspicion, who was set over them matters nothing.—But still in reality he only discharged the servile duty of providing them with arms.—But he never was set over them, and that duty was always discharged by Bellus, a freedman of Faustus.

CHAPTER XX.

56. BUT Sittius was sent by him into further Spain, to stir up that province. In the first place, O judges,

Sittius set out when L. Julius and C. Figulus were consuls, sometime before this frenzy of Cataline's, and (before there was any) suspicion of this conspiracy : in the second place he set out not then for the first time, but after he had been several years in the same places some time before for the same purpose : and he set out not only with an object, but even with a necessary object, having a large account to settle with the king of Mauritania. But then, when he was gone, as Sulla managed his affairs and carried them on, very many and (some) most beautiful farms of P. Sittius were sold, and (thus) his debts were paid ; so that the motive which drove the rest to this wickedness, (namely) the desire of retaining their possessions, this did not exist in (the case of) Sittius, since his farms were diminished.

57. But now how incredible is this, how absurd, that a man who wished to make a massacre at Rome, who wished to burn this city, that he should send away from him his own most intimate friend, and remove to the most distant countries ! Whether (did he do so) in order that he might effect more easily at Rome those things which he was attempting, if there were seditions in Spain ? But these very things were done independently (*per se*) and without any connexion. Did he then think that in (the midst of) affairs so important, in plans so novel, so dangerous, so seditious, he ought to send away a man thoroughly attached to himself, his own most intimate friend, one thoroughly connected with him by duties, intercourse, habit ? It is not probable, that, the very man whom in prosperity, whom in tranquility he had always had with him, this same man, in adversity and in that tumult which he himself had raised, he should send away from him.

58. But (is) Sittius himself,—for I must not desert the cause of my old friend and host,—(is he) such a man, or is that family and school such, that this can be believed, that he wished to make war on the Roman people ? (can we believe)

that (he) whose father, when other borderers and neighbours revolted (from us), behaved with singular duty and good faith toward our republic, (that) he should think that a nefarious war ought to be undertaken by him against his country? (A man) whose debts we see, (O judges), were contracted, not through lust, but from a desire to extend his business: who owed debts at Rome so that large sums of money were due to him in the provinces and the kingdoms, and when he applied for them he did not allow his agent to be put to any difficulty through his absence; but preferred to sell all his possessions, and himself to be stripped of a most beautiful patrimony, rather than that any delay should be caused to any of his creditors.

59. Of which class (of men), O judges, I never had any fear, when I was living in that tempest of the republic. That class of men was formidable and terrible, who clung to and held their possessions with such affection, that you would say that their limbs could more quickly be torn from them and dragged away (than their property). Sittius never thought that there was any relationship between him and his estates. Therefore he cleared himself not only from the suspicion of so great wickedness, but even from all talk of men, not by arms but by his patrimony.

CHAPTER XXI.

60. BUT now, as to the objection he makes, that the people of Pompeii were excited by Sulla to join that conspiracy and to this abominable wickedness, of what sort that statement is I cannot understand. Do the people of Pompeii appear to you to have joined the conspiracy? Who has ever said this? or what even slightest suspicion was there of this fact? "He separated them," he says, "from the

settlers, in order that when this division and dissension was made, he might be able to have the town in his power through the people of Pompeii." In the first place, the whole dissension between the natives of Pompeii and the settlers was referred to the patrons, since already it was of long standing and had been agitated for many years : in the second place the matter was investigated by the patrons in such a way, that Sulla did not in any particular dissent from the opinions of the others : lastly the settlers themselves so understand (it), that the natives of Pompeii were not defended by Sulla more than they themselves (were).

61. And this, O judges, you may understand from this numerous attendance of the settlers, most honourable men, who are present, who are anxious : they desire that this man, the patron, the defender, the guardian of that colony, if they have not been able to hold him safe in every (sort of) good-fortune, and in every honour, yet, in this present misfortune, in which he lies attacked, he may be assisted and preserved by you. The natives of Pompeii are here also with equal eagerness, who are summoned by them (the prosecutors) also on the charge : who have differed with the settlers about walks and about their votes (only) to such an extent that they (still) think the same about the common safety.

62. And this virtue indeed of P. Sulla seems to me (to be one which ought) not to be passed over in silence, that, although that colony was settled by him, and though the fortune of the republic has separated the interests of the colonists from the fortunes of the natives of Pompeii, (yet) he (Sulla) is so dear to both parties, and (so) popular, that he does not seem to have removed the one party (from their lands) but to have settled both.

CHAPTER XXII.

"But (you say) "the gladiators and all that violence

was prepared on account of the motion of Cæcilius." And yet he bitterly inveighed, in this place against L. Cæcilius, a most virtuous and most accomplished man : of whose virtue and constancy, O judges, I say only thus much, that he behaved in such a manner in that motion which he brought forward, not about doing away with, but about lightening the misfortune of his brother, that (although) he wished to consult for (the interest of) his brother, (yet) he was unwilling to be at variance with the republic : he proposed it urged on by brotherly affection, he abandoned it led by the authority of his brother.

63. And in that matter Sulla is accused by L. Cæcilius, in which both ought to be praised : in the first place Cæcilius, for if he proposed that in which he seemed to have wished to rescind legal decisions, (namely) that Sulla should be restored, you rightly blame (him) : for the stability of the republic is especially supported by legal decisions : nor do I think that so much is to be yielded to love for a brother, that anyone, while he consults for the safety of his own relations, should relinquish the common (safety). But he brought forward no proposition about the decision, but he did away with that punishment for bribery which had been lately established by former laws. Therefore by this motion, not the decision of the judges, but a defect in the law was sought to be corrected. No one blames the legal decision, but the law, when he complains of the penalty. For the conviction is the act of the judges, which remains : the penalty is the act of the law, which may be lightened.

64. Be unwilling therefore to alienate from your cause the inclinations of those orders (of men) who preside over the courts with authority and dignity. No one has attempted to weaken the decision, nothing of that sort has been proposed : in the calamity of his brother Cæcilius always thought that the power of the judges ought to be preserved but that the severity of the law ought to be mitigated.

CHAPTER XXIII.

BUT why do I argue further about this ? I might speak perhaps, and I would speak easily and gladly, if affection and fraternal love had impelled L. Cæcilius even a little further than the limit of regular duty requires : I might implore your feelings : I might call to witness the indulgence which every one feels for his own relatives : I might seek pardon for the fault of L. Cæcilius from your own inmost thoughts, and from common humanity.

65. The law was proposed (only) a few days : it was never begun to be carried, it was deposited in the senate. On the 1st of January, when we had summoned the senate to the Capitol, nothing took precedence of it, and Q. Metullus the prætor said that he said this by command of Sulla, that Sulla was unwilling that such a proposal should be brought forward concerning him. From that time L. Cæcilius trans- acted many measures for the (good of) the republic : he declared that he would be a protester against the agrarian law, which had been entirely blamed and rejected by me, he resisted infamous bribery, he never hindered the authority of the senate, he so behaved himself in his tribuneship, that, laying aside the burden of domestic duty, he thought of nothing afterwards except the welfare of the republic.

66. And in this very proposal, who at that time of us feared Sulla or Cæcilius lest they should attempt to carry anything by violence ? Did not all that terror, all fear and expectation of sedition rest upon the villany of Autronius ? His expressions, his threats were reported ; the sight of him, the running together (of people to escort him), the crowding, the bands of his abandoned followers, brought to us fear and sedition. Therefore P. Sulla, since this most troublesome man was his partner and companion, both in honour and also in calamity, was compelled to lose (his own) good fortune, and to remain in adversity without any remedy or alleviation.

CHAPTER XXIV.

67. AT this point you often recite (passages from) my letter, which I sent to Cn. Pompeius about my own achievements, and about the highest interests of the republic, and from it you seek some charge against P. Sulla ; and, because I wrote that an incredible mad attempt, conceived two years before, had broken out in my consulship, you say that I by this expression have proved, that Sulla was in that former conspiracy. Forsooth (I suppose) I am such a man as to think that Cn. Piso and Cataline and Vargunteius and Autronius could do nothing wickedly, nothing boldly by themselves without P. Sulla.

68. About which point even if auyone had doubted previously, whether he had thought of this, which you accuse him of, (namely), after the murder of your father, to descend (into the Campus Martius) as consul on the first of January with the lictors, you have removed this suspicion, when you said that he (Sulla), in order to make Cataline Consul, had cherished designs and prepared an armed band against your father. And if I should grant this to you, then you must necessarily grant to me, that he (Sulla), when he was voting for Cataline, had no thoughts of recovering by violence his own consulship which he had lost by a judicial decision.

However the character of P. Sulla is not liable to the charge of such great, such atrocious crimes, O judges.

69. For now I shall proceed, having disposed of almost all the charges against him, contrary to the arrangement which is wont to be observed in other cases, to speak now at last about the life of my client, and about his habits. For at the beginning my mind was eager to meet the magnitude of the charge, to satisfy the expectations of men, to say something of my own self, because I had been accused : now you must be called back to that point, to which the cause itself, even if I were silent, compels you to turn your mind and attention.

E

CHAPTER XXV.

In all matters, O judges, which are more serious and more important, we must consider what each one has wished, has intended, has done, not from the charge, but from the habit of the person who is accused. For no one of us can be suddenly formed (in character), nor can the life or nature of anyone be suddenly changed or altered.

70. Survey briefly in your own minds, to pass over other instances, these very men who were implicated in this wickedness. Cataline conspired against the republic. Whose ears ever disbelieved this, that a man had made this bold attempt, (who) from his boyhood had been versed, not only in intemperance and wickedness, but even by habit and desire in every kind of crime, lust and bloodshed? Who wonders that that man perished fighting against his country, whom all always thought born for a civil robbery? Who that recollects the partnerships of Lentulus with informers, (who that recollects) the insanity of his lusts, his perverse and impious superstition, will wonder that he either cherished wicked designs or entertained foolish hopes? Who thinks of C. Cethegus and his expedition into Spain, and of the wound of Q. Metellus Pius, to whom a prison does not seem to have been built for his punishment.

71. I pass over others, lest there should be no end (to my examples). I only ask of you silently to think of all those men who are known to have conspired: you will perceive that every one of them was condemned by his own life before (he was condemned) by our suspicion. As for that Autronius himself, since his name is most nearly connected with the danger and charge against my client (*hujus*), did not his own life and nature convict him? (He was) always audacious, violent, profligate, (a man) whom in defending himself (against charges of adultery) we know to have been accustomed to use not only most infamous language, but even

his fists and his feet, a man who (was wont) to drive men from their possessions, to cause the murder of his neighbours, to plunder the temples of the allies, to disturb the courts by violence and arms, in prosperity to despise everybody, in adversity to fight against (all) good men, not to yield to (the interests of) the republic, not to succumb to fortune herself. If his case were not made clear by most irresistible evidence, yet his own habits and life would convict him.

CHAPTER XXVI.

72.   COME then, compare now with his (life) the life of P. Sulla, well known to you and the Roman people, O judges, and place it before your eyes. Is there any act or deed of his, I will not say somewhat audacious, but which has seemed to anyone a little too inconsiderate? Any deed do I ask? Has any word even fallen from his mouth, at which anyone could be offended? Even in that serious and disorderly victory of L. Sulla, who was found more gentle than P. Sulla who more merciful? How many men's lives did he beg from L. Sulla! How many men are there of the highest rank and most accomplished, both of our order and of the equestrian order, for whose safety he laid himself under obligations to Sulla! Whom I might name—for they themselves are not unwilling, and they are present to (countenance) him with most grateful feelings—but because that service is greater than one citizen ought to be able to grant to another, therefore I beg of you to impute to the opportunity what he was able (to do), to himself, what he did.

73.   Why need I mention the remaining firmness of his life, his dignity, liberality, moderation in private affairs, his splendour on public occasions? Which (virtues) have been so crippled by fortune, as yet to appear to have had their foundations laid by nature. What a house (was his)? What a daily

crowd (frequented it), what dignity (he showed) to his acquaintances, what attachment (was there to him on the part) of his friends, what a multitude (of them he had) of every rank! These things, obtained by long time and much labour, one hour snatched away. P. Sulla received, O judges, a wound terrible and mortal, but yet of such a sort as his life and nature seemed to have been able to receive. He was judged to have had too great a desire for honour and dignity, which if no one else had in standing for the consulship, then he is to be judged to have been more covetous than the rest; but if also in some others there was that desire for the consulship, fortune in his case was perhaps more severe than to others.

74. But afterwards who saw P. Sulla otherwise than grieving, dejected, cast down? Who ever suspected that he was avoiding the sight of men and the light more through hatred than through shame? For when he had many inducements to (visit) this city and forum, on account of the very great attachment of his friends, which yet remained to him the sole (consolation) in his misfortunes, he kept out of your sight, and, when by law he could have remained, he almost condemned himself to banishment.

CHAPTER XXVII.

IN this modest conduct, O judges, and in such a life, do you believe there was room for so great wickedness? Look at the man himself, behold his countenance, compare the charge with his life, compare with the charge his life (which has been) laid open (to you) even to this day.

75. I say nothing of the republic, which was always most dear to Sulla : did he wish those friends (of his), (being) such men (as they are), so attached to him, by whom his prosperity formerly had been adorned, (by whom) his adversity is now lightened, to perish most miserably, that, in company with Lentulus and Cataline and Cethegus, he might pass a

most infamous and miserable life with a most disgraceful death set before him ? That suspicion, I say, does not fall in with such habits, with such a life (as his), nor with the man himself. That sprang up as it were a new sort of barbarity, it was an incredible and singular madness; that so great foulness of unheard of wickedness blazed up suddenly from the many vices of abandoned men accumulated from their youth.

76. Be not willing, O judges, to think that to have been the violence and attempt of human beings; for no nation ever was so barbarous or so savage, in which, not only so many, but even one so cruel an enemy of his country could be found : they were some savage and wild beasts, (sprung) from monsters, clothed in the form of men. Look again and again, O judges, for there is nothing which in this cause can be asserted too vehemently, look deeply into the minds of Cataline, Autronius, Cethegus, Lentulus, and the rest : what lusts you will find in these men, what crimes, what baseness, what audacity, what incredible madness, what marks of wickedness, what traces of parricide, what heaps of guilt ! Out of the great and long-standing and now desperate diseases of the republic that violence suddenly broke out, (in such a way) that, when it was finished and got rid of, the state might at length become convalescent and be cured ; for there is not anyone who thinks, that if those pests were included in the republic this (republic) could any longer exist. Therefore some furies urged them on, not to carry out their wickedness, but to pay a penalty to the republic.

CHAPTER XXVIII.

77. INTO this band will you now, O judges, cast P. Sulla, from out of those bands of most honourable men, who are living and have lived with him ? Will you transfer him from this number of friends, from this dignity of his intimates, to

the party of impious men, and to the abode and number of parricides ? Where then will be that most impregnable defence of modesty ? In what place will the previous deeds of our life profit us ? To what time will the reward of a character (already) gained be reserved, if it shall desert him in his utmost need and contest with fortune, if it shall not stand by him, if it shall give him no help ?

78. The prosecutor threatens us with the examinations and tortures of our slaves. And although we suspect no danger from these, yet pain reigns in those tortures, it is regulated by each one's nature, both of mind and body, the inquisitor rules, caprice sways (them), hope corrupts (them), fear weakens (them), so that in such straits no place is left for truth. Let the life of P. Sulla be put to the torture; from it let enquiry be made whether any lust is concealed, whether any crime is lying hid, whether any cruelty, whether any audacity. There will be nothing of mistake in the cause, nor of obscurity, O Judges, if the voice of his whole life, which is most true, and ought to be of the greatest weight, shall be listened to by you. In this cause we fear no witness ; we think that no one knows, no one has seen, no one has heard anything (to harm us).

79. But however, if the fortune of P. Sulla in no way moves you, O judges, let your own move you. For in your (fortune), who have lived in the greatest elegance and integrity, this is of the greatest importance, that the causes of honourable men should not be weighed according to caprice, or enmity, or worthlessness, but that in important investigations and sudden dangers, the life of each one should be a witness. And do not you, O judges, be willing to give up to envy, and to abandon to suspicion, this (life) stripped of its arms and laid bare. Fortify the common citadel of good men, block up the refuges of the wicked, let that (witness) avail the most both for punishment and for safety, which alone you see can most easily be examined by itself from its own nature, which cannot be suddenly altered or modelled.

CHAPTER XXIX.

80. WHAT indeed? Shall this authority, for I must continually speak of that, although it shall be spoken of by me timidly and moderately, what, I say, shall this authority of mine, who have kept aloof from other cases of conspiracy, who am defending P. Sulla, be of no avail to my client forsooth? This is a serious thing to say perhaps, O judges, a serious thing, if we are asking anything; if, when others are silent about us, we are not also ourselves silent, it is a serious thing: but, if we are attacked, if we are accused, if we are called into unpopularity, surely you grant, O judges, that it should be allowed us to retain our liberty, if it be not quite allowed us (to retain) our dignity.

81. (All) the men of consular rank are accused under one accusation, so that now the name of greatest honour seems to bring more unpopularity than dignity. "They countenanced "Cataline," says he, "and praised him." At that time no conspiracy was discovered, none was known of: they were defending a friend, they were countenancing a suppliant, in his most imminent danger they did not censure the infamy of his life. Moreover even your father, O Torquatus, when consul, was advocate for Cataline as defendant on a charge of extortion, a wicked man, but a suppliant, audacious perhaps, but once a friend. And since he countenanced him after that first conspiracy had been disclosed to him, he showed that he had heard something, but had not believed it. "But he did not "countenance him at the other trial, when the rest counte-"nanced him." If he himself had afterwards learnt something, of which during his consulship he had been ignorant, we must pardon those who after that time heard nothing; but if that first accusation had weight, whether ought it to be more weighty when old than when fresh? But if your father, even in the suspicion itself of danger to himself, yet induced by

humanity did honour to the defence of a most worthless man
by his curule chair and by dignities both his own and (those)
of his consulship, what reason is there why the men of consular
rank, who countenanced Cataline, should be blamed ?

82. "But the same man did not countenance those, who
"before this case, were accused of conspiracy." They resolved
that to men implicated in such great wickedness, no support,
no help, no assistance ought to be given by them. And—that
I may speak of the constancy and attachment to the republic
of those whose silent dignity and loyalty speaks in behalf of
each one, and needs not the ornaments of language from
anyone,—can anyone say that there ever were men of consular
rank more virtuous, more brave, more firm, than (those who
lived) in those times and dangers, in which the republic was
almost overwhelmed ? Who did not give his thoughts for the
common safety to the best of his ability, most bravely, most
firmly ? Nor do I argue chiefly about men of consular rank ;
for this credit is common to (all) those accomplished men, who
were prætors, and to the whole senate in common, so that it is
evident that, since the memory of man, never was there in that
order more virtue, more attachment to the republic, more
weight : but because men of consular rank were specially
mentioned, I thought I ought to say thus much concerning
them, which might suffice to call to witness the memory of all,
that there was no one of that rank of honour, who did not,
with all his zeal, virtue, and influence, labour to preserve the
republic.

CHAPTER XXX.

83. But what (shall) I (say) ? I who never praised
Cataline, who as consul never countenanced Cataline when on
trial, I who gave evidence concerning the conspiracy against
others, do I seem to you so far removed from sanity, so
forgetful of my own consistency, so unmindful of my exploits,

that, when as consul I waged war with the conspirators, now I
should wish to preserve their leader, and to bring my mind
now to defend the cause and life of that man whose weapon I
lately blunted, and whose flame I extinguished? If, by the
God of truth (*medius fidius*), O judges, the republic itself,
preserved by my labours and dangers, could not recall me by
its dignity to firmness of mind and consistency, yet this is
implanted by nature, always to hate him whom you have
feared, with whom you have contended for life and fortune,
from whose plots you have escaped. But when my chiefest
honour is at stake, and the conspicuous glory of my exploits,
when, as often as anyone is convicted (of complicity) in this
wickedness, so often the recollection of the safety of the city
having been secured by me is renewed, can I be so mad, can I
allow those things which I did for the safety of all, to appear
to have been done by me by chance and good-fortune more
than by virtue and wisdom? "What then? Do you claim
this for yourself," perhaps some one will say, "that because you
"defend a man, he shall be judged innocent?" I indeed, O
judges, not only claim nothing to myself to which anyone can
object, but even, if anything is granted by all, that I give up
and abandon. I am not living in such a republic, I have not
exposed my life at such times to all sorts of dangers for my
country, those whom I have defeated are not so extinct, nor
those whom I have preserved so grateful, that I should
endeavour to assume to myself more than as much as all my
enemies and enviers may endure.

84. It seems a serious thing for him who investigated
the conspiracy, who laid it open, who crushed it, whom the
senate thanked in unprecedented language, who is the only
citizen to whom it decreed a supplication, to say in a court of
justice, "I would not have defended him, if he had been a
conspirator." I do not say that, because it is a serious thing
(to say): I say this, which in these cases of conspiracy I can
assume, not to my influence, but to my modesty: I, the

F

investigator and chastiser of the conspiracy, certainly would
not defend Sulla, if I thought he had been a conspirator.
I, O judges, when I was making enquiry into all things
concerning these so great dangers of all, heard many things,
did not believe all, was cautious about everything, I say this,
which I said at the beginning, that no matter was brought
before me concerning P. Sulla, by the information of anyone,
(or) by the message of anyone, (or) by the suspicion of anyone.

CHAPTER XXXI.

86. WHEREFORE, you, O Gods of my country and of my
household, who preside over this city and this republic, who
have preserved this empire, this liberty (of ours), and the
Roman people, and these houses and temples, when I was
consul, by your authority and assistance, (you) I call to
witness, that I, with an honest and free mind, am defending
the cause of P. Sulla, that no crime is concealed by me
knowingly, that no wickedness undertaken against the safety
of all is being defended and covered. As consul I found out
nothing about this man, I suspected nothing, I heard
nothing.

87. Therefore I that same person who have seemed
vehement against some, inexorable against others, paid my
country what I owed (to her): the rest now is due to my
constant habit and nature; I am as merciful, O judges,
as you, as gentle as he who is the most soft-hearted. In
whatever I was vehement together with you, I did nothing
unless compelled: I came to the assistance of the republic
when in danger, I raised up my country when sinking; in-
fluenced by pity for the citizens I was then as vehement as
was necessary. The safety of all would have been lost in one
night, if that severity had not been exercised. But as I was

led on to the punishment of wicked men by love for the republic, so I am led on to the safety of the innocent by my inclination.

88. I see nothing, O judges, in this P. Sulla, worthy of hatred, many things deserving of pity : for he does not now, O judges, flee to you as a suppliant for the sake of warding off his own calamity, but that no stigma of nefarious baseness may be branded on his family and name. For he himself indeed, if he shall be liberated by your decision, what honours will he have, what solaces for the rest of his life, which he can rejoice in and enjoy ? His house, I suppose, will be adorned, the images of his ancestors will be displayed, he himself will resume his ornaments and former dress. All these, O judges, are lost; all the insignia and ornaments of his family, his name, his honour have fallen by the calamity of one decision. But, lest he should be called the destroyer of his country, its betrayer, its enemy, lest he should leave this disgrace of so great a crime to his family, that he is anxious about, that he fears ; lest forsooth this unhappy (child) should be called the son of a conspirator, and a criminal, and a traitor. For this boy he fears, who is much dearer to him than his own life, that if he is not likely to hand down to him the undiminished fruits of honour, (yet) he may not leave him the eternal recollection of disgrace.

89. This little child entreats you, O judges, to permit him sometimes to congratulate his father, if not with unimpaired fortune, yet in his afflicted (fortune) ; to this unhappy boy the roads to the courts and the forum are better known than those to the Campus Martius and the Schools. I am not now contending, O judges, about the life of P. Sulla, but about his burial : life was snatched (from him) by a former decision, now we are striving that his body may not be cast out. For what is left to him, which can detain him in this life, or what is there on account of which this can seem life to any one.

CHAPTER XXXII.

Lately P. Sulla was such a man in the state, that no-one thought himself superior to him in honour, or in influence, or in good-fortune : now, stripped of all his dignity, he does not seek back what has been taken away; that little which fortune has left him in his disasters, (namely) that he may be permitted to bewail his calamity with his parent, with his children, with his brother, with his friends, that he begs of you, O judges, not to snatch from him.

90. It were fitting for you yourself now, O Torquatus, to be satisfied with the miseries of my client : although you should have taken nothing else from Sulla but the consulship, yet you ought to be content with that; for a contest for honour, not enmity, led you to (undertake) this cause. But since, together with honour, everything has been taken from him, since, in this most miserable and most grievous fortune, he is desolate, what is there which you can ask for more ? Do you wish to snatch (from him) this enjoyment of the light (of day), full (as it is) of tears and of grief, in which he is retained in the greatest torment and pain ? He would gladly give it up, if the ignominy of a most odious charge were taken away. Or indeed (do you seek) to banish him as an enemy ? From his miseries, if you were most hard-hearted, you would derive greater pleasure in seeing (them) than in hearing (of them).

91. O wretched and unhappy day, on which P. Sulla was declared consul by all the centuries, O false hope, O fleeting fortune, O blind cupidity, O unreasonable congratulation ! How quickly all those things fell back from joy and pleasure to grief and tears, so that he, who a short time before had been consul elect, suddenly retained no trace of his former dignity ! For what evil was there which seemed to be wanting to him, when stripped of fame, honour, fortune, or was any room left for any new calamity ? The same fortune

pursues him which pursued him at first; she finds new grief; she does not suffer an unfortunate man to perish afflicted by one evil, in one grief (only).

CHAPTER XXXIII.

92. But now I myself am hindered, O judges, by grief of mind, from saying more about the miseries of my client. It is now your part, O judges; on your mercy and humanity I rest the whole cause. You, a rejection (of several judges) having been interposed, of which we had no suspicion, have sat as judges suddenly appointed for us, chosen by our accusers through their hope of your severity, appointed by fortune for us to protect our innocence. As I have been anxious, as to what the Roman people thought of me, because I was severe towards the wicked, and (therefore) have undertaken the first defence of an innocent man which was offered to me, so do you mitigate that severity of the courts, which for some months has been exerted against most audacious men, by your lenity and mercy.

93. The cause itself ought to obtain this from you, and it is (the part) of your virtue and courage to declare, that you are not those to whom it is desirable to apply after a rejection (of other judges) has been interposed. In which matter I, O judges, as far as my affection for you demands, so far I exhort you, with common zeal, since we are united in (the service of) the republic, (and) by your humanity and mercy, to repel from us the false reputation of cruelty.

J. Hall & Son, Printers, Cambridge.

J. HALL and SON'S

LIST OF

EDUCATIONAL WORKS.

---—∞◇∞——

STUDENTS' EDITIONS OF THE GOSPELS & THE ACTS.

THE GOSPEL of S. MATTHEW;

The Greek Text, with Critical, Grammatical, and Explanatory Notes, &c., by the late Rev. W. TROLLOPE, M.A., *new Edition*, thoroughly revised and re-edited by the Rev. W. H. ROWLANDSON, M.A., late Fellow and Divinity Lecturer at Corpus Christi College, Cambridge. cr. 8vo cloth, 5/-

GOSPEL of S. MARK;

The Greek Text, with Critical, Grammatical, and Explanatory Notes, Prolegomena, &c., by Rev. W. H. ROWLANDSON, M.A. *2nd Edition.* cr. 8vo. cloth, 4/6

GOSPEL of S. LUKE;

The Greek Text, with Critical, Grammatical and Explanatory Notes, &c. by the late Rev. W. Trollope, M.A., *new Edition*, thoroughly revised and re-edited by the Rev. W. H. ROWLANDSON, M.A., cr. 8vo cloth, 5/-

ACTS OF THE APOSTLES;

The Greek Text, with Critical, Grammatical, and Explanatory Notes, and Examination Questions, by Rev. W. Trollope, M.A., *new Edition*, re-edited and thoroughly revised by the Rev. G. F. BROWNE, M.A., late Fellow and Assistant Tutor of S. Catharine's College. cr. 8vo. cloth, 5/-

---

COMPENDIUM THEOLOGICUM, or Manual for Students

in THEOLOGY: containing a CONCISE HISTORY of the Primitive and Mediæval Church, — The Reformation,—The Church of England,—The English Liturgy, and the XXXIX Articles, with Scripture Proofs and Explanations; by the Rev. O. ADOLPHUS, M.A. *Fifth Edition.* Considerably Enlarged. cr. 8vo. *cloth*, 8/6

MICAH; A New Translation,

With Notes for English Readers and Hebrew Students, by JOHN SHARPE, M.A., late Fellow and Lecturer of Christ's College. Cr. 8vo cloth, 5/-

J. HALL & SON'S PUBLICATIONS.

ORDINATION QUESTIONS,

Being the Papers given at Recent Examinations both for Deacons and Priests, together with Instructions to Candidates. Fscp. 8vo 2/-

....

SCHOOL AND UNIVERSITY ANALYSES.

By the Rev. Dr. PINNOCK.

SCRIPTURE HISTORY;

An Analysis of, Intended for Readers of OLD TESTAMENT HISTORY, and the University Examinations; with MAPS, *Copious Index, and Examination Questions. New Edit.* 18mo. cloth, 3/6

NEW TESTAMENT HISTORY;

An Analysis of, Embracing the Criticism and Interpretation of the original Text; *with Questions for Examination. New Edition.* 18mo. cloth, 4/-

ECCLESIASTICAL HISTORY;

An Analysis of, From the Birth of Christ, to the Council of Nice, A. D. 325. *With Examination Questions. Eighth Edition, improved,* 18mo. cloth, 3/6

ENGLISH CHURCH HISTORY;

Analysis of, comprising the REFORMATION period, and subsequent events; with *Questions of Examination,* especially intended for the Universities, and Divinity Students in general. *Seventh Edition.* 18mo. cloth, 4/6

A SHORT ANALYSIS of OLD TESTAMENT HISTORY,

with *Questions for Schools. Eighth Edition.* 18mo. cloth, 1/6

A SHORT ANALYSIS of NEW TESTAMENT HISTORY,

with *Questions for Schools. Second Edition.* 18mo cloth, 1/6

THE LAW OF THE RUBRIC;

and the Transition Period of the CHURCH of ENGLAND, 8vo *sewed,* 3/-

The CHURCH KEY, BELFRY KEY, and ORGAN KEY;

with Legal Cases, and Opinions, PARISH LAY COUNCILS, and the AUTOCRACY of the CLERGY. 8vo cloth, 5/-

RUBRICS FOR COMMUNICANTS;

Explanatory of the HOLY COMMUNION OFFICE, with Prayers, Aids to Examination, and Scripture Illustrations, (to be used in Churches). 18mo. cloth, 1/-

CHURCH CHOIRS AND CHURCH MUSIC;

Their Origin and Usefulness. *Second Edition.* 8vo. *sewed,* 6d

J. HALL & SON'S PUBLICATIONS.

DR. PINNOCK'S WORKS, continued:—

CLERICAL PAPERS——Laws and Usages of the Church
and Clergy;
6 vols. cr. 8vo. cloth; each Volume complete in its own
subject, and may be had *separately:*—

The Curate and Unbeneficed Clerk (*Second Edition*)...... VOL. A. 5/6
The Officiating Minister ....(ditto)............... VOL. B. 5/6
The Ornaments of the Church ....(ditto)............... VOL. C. 6/6
The Ornaments of the Minister................................... VOL. D. 5/6
The Order and Ritual of Public Worship, Morning } VOL. E. 5/6
   Prayer .... }
Evening Prayer, Litany, and The Holy Communion VOL. F. 6/6
   (the concluding Volume) ....

BY THE REV. J. GORLE, M. A.

BUTLER'S ANALOGY, a New Analysis of,
  With *Questions. Fourth Edition.* 18mo cloth, 3/-

PEARSON ON THE CREED; an Analysis of,
  with *Examination Questions. Fifth Edition.* 18mo cloth, 4/-

HOOKER, Book V., an Analysis of,
  With *Examination Questions. Third Edition.* 18mo cloth, 4/-

PALEY'S HORÆ PAULINÆ, an Analysis of,
  with *Examination Questions,* together with a Tabular Outline of
  St Paul's Life. *Second Edition.* 18mo. cloth, 3/-

BY THE REV. W. TROLLOPE, M.A.

LITURGY and RITUAL of the CHURCH of ENGLAND,
a Practical and Historical Commentary on the;
  With copious *Examination Questions. Second Edition.*
  Cr. 8vo cloth, 5/-

    "To enable Divinity Students and Candidates for Holy Orders to master this
    important branch of Theological Learning the above is admirably
    adapted...........We hope it will be brought into extensive use."—
    Literary Churchman.

XXXIX ARTICLES of the CHURCH of ENGLAND;
  Questions and Answers on the. *Sixth Edition, Improved and
  enlarged.* 18mo cloth, 2/6

LITURGY of the CHURCH of ENGLAND;
  Questions and Answers on the. *Ninth Edition.* 18mo cloth, 2/-

EXAMINATION QUESTIONS ON THE PENTATEUCH.
  Fcp. 8vo cloth 1/-

JUSTINI PHILOSOPHI et MARTYRIS cum TRYPHONE
  Judæo Dialogus, edited with a corrected Text. English Intro-
  duction, Notes, and Indices. By the late Rev. W. TROL-
  LOPE, M.A. 8vo. 6/-

WAKE'S APOSTOLICAL EPISTLES;

Being the genuine EPISTLES of the APOSTOLICAL FATHERS; translated by WILLIAM WAKE, D.D., late Archbishop of Canterbury. *New Edition*, carefully revised. cr. 8vo. cloth, 5/-

PALEY'S EVIDENCES OF CHRISTIANITY;

Comprising the Text of Paley, verbatim; *Examination Questions* at the foot of each page, and a full Analysis prefixed to each Chapter. By Rev. GEORGE FISK, LL.B. Prebendary of Lichfield. *Sixth Edition.* cr. 8vo cloth, 4/6

PALEY'S EVIDENCES OF CHRISTIANITY,

A Short Analysis of, with Questions, and recent *Examination Papers*, by the Rev. J. M. BACON, B.A., Scholar of Trinity College, Cambridge. *Second Edition.* 18mo cloth. 2/6

The aim of this Analysis has been to give a thoroughly comprehensive digest of the Original Work, and at the same time to render it as concise as possible, so that the memory may retain the important points of Paley's Argument without being burdened with too much detail.

PALEY'S EVIDENCES OF CHRISTIANITY; the Argument

of, Intended for the use of Candidates for the Previous Examinations, as a Companion to the entire Work of Paley. *Second Edition.* 18mo. 1/-

THE CREED AND THE CHURCH; a Hand-Book of

THEOLOGY; being a SYNOPSIS of Pearson on the Creed; and of Hooker's Ecclesiastical Polity, Book V., with brief Papers on Heresies and Schisms; Life and Epistles of St. Paul; History of the Book of Common Prayer; XXXIX Articles, &c., by the REV. EDGAR SANDERSON, M.A., late Scholar of Clare College. *Third Edition.* Post 8vo. cloth, 3/6

"A very miracle of condensation. It includes within the limits of 240 pages of very small 8vo. a synopsis of Pearson on the Creed, and Hooker's Ecclesiastical Polity, Book V, and brief papers on Heresies and Schisms, the Life and Epistles of St. Paul, the History of the Book of Common Prayer, the Thirty-nine Articles, and the first four General Councils.—The abridgment is so fairly done, especially in the case of Pearson, as to retain a well-proportioned resemblance to the argument of the original.—*Critique* in "*Contemporary Review.*"

OLD TESTAMENT HISTORY;

In the form of Question & Answer, by R. J. Griffiths, B.A., LL.B., 18mo cloth, 9d.

GROTIUS (Hugo) on the Truth of the Christian Religion,

translated by Dr. JOHN CLARKE, with Notes; a *New Edition.* cr. 8vo. cl. 3/-

HALLAM'S CONSTITUTIONAL HISTORY of ENGLAND,

An Analysis of : For the use of Students, with Tables, Explanation of Terms, &c., by GEORGE PARKER, B.A. St. John's College, cr. 8vo 3/6

BOOK OF HINTS for the CAMBRIDGE "PREVIOUS" & "GENERAL" EXAMINATIONS,

Containing Paley Verses, The Synoptic Gospels, Acts of the Apostles, Important Formulæ in Trigonometry, Mechanics, and Hydrostatics. Fscp. 8vo 1/-

J. HALL & SON'S PUBLICATIONS.

A New ELEMENTARY GRAMMAR, of the HEBREW LANGUAGE.
By P. H. MASON, M.A., Fellow & Hebrew Lecturer, of St. John's College. Second Edition, 8vo cloth, 5/6. Key to ditto, 3/6

HEBREW EXERCISE BOOK,
Consisting of an Outline of Hebrew Grammar with Progressive Exercises, (Hebrew English, and English Hebrew): by P. H. MASON, M.A., St. John's College. *Second Edit.* 8vo cloth, 18/- Key to ditto, 4/6

SHEMETS DAVAR,
A Rabbinic Reading Book, illustrating some Rabbinic modes of expression and thought, by P. H. MASON, M.A., 8vo *cloth*, 10/6

LATIN AND GREEK ACCIDENCE,
Intended chiefly for the Use of Candidates for the *Previous Examinations* at Cambridge, and the Military Examinations: by J. PERKINS, M. A., Fellow and Tutor of Downing College. *Fifth Edition.* or. 8vo cloth, 3/6

SYNOPSIS OF LATIN ACCIDENCE,
on a Sheet, price 6d.

LUSUS ACADEMICI;
A Selection of Translations, chiefly from the English Poets, into Greek and Latin Verse, by T. A. MARSHALL, M.A., Principal of Milford College. cr. 8vo. cloth, 4/-

ARISTOPHANES, The Birds of,
Literally Translated with Notes, by W. C. GREEN, M.A. late Fellow of King's College, Assistant Master at Rugby, cr. 8vo 2/6

ARISTOPHANES, The Clouds of
Literally Translated with Notes, by W. C. GREEN, M.A. cr. 8vo 2/6

ÆSCHYLI PERSÆ,
a *Literal Translation* of, 12mo *sewed*, 1/-

ÆSCHYLI PROMETHEUS VINCTUS;
The Test with *English Notes and Literal Translation*, by J. PERKINS, M.A. Fellow and Tutor of Downing College. Interleaved, 12mo cloth, 3/6. The Translation only sewed, 1/-

ARISTOTLE'S NICOMACHEAN ETHICS, Books V & X,
Translated, with a Revised Greek Text, and Brief Explanatory Notes, by F. A. PALEY, M. A., 12mo cloth, 4/-

CICERO PRO ARCHIA, ET PRO BALBO,
Literally Translated, with Notes, by P. H. CLIFFORD, B. A., Christ's College. Cr. 8vo 3/-

CICERO'S ORATIONS AGAINST CATILINA:
Translated into English, with Notes, by W. C. Green, M.A. cr. 8vo 2/6

CICERO PRO CLUENTIO;
> a new *Literal Translation*, with Notes, by the Rev. W. C. GREEN, M.A. late Fellow of King's College, Assistant Master at Rugby. *Second Edition.* Cr. 8vo 2/6

CICERO DE LEGIBUS,
> the Text, revised and explained, by W. D. PEARMAN, M.A., S. Peter's College, cr. 8vo 4/6

CICERO PRO LEGE MANILIA;
> *Literally Translated* by C. H. CROSSE, M.A. & M.L. cr. 8vo 2/6

CICERO PRO MILONE;
> *Translated into Literal English.* By a Graduate. 12mo *sewed*, 1/-

CICERO PRO MURENA,
> With *English Notes* and a *Literal Translation*, by H. REYNOLDS, M.A., cr. 8vo 2/6

DEMOSTHENES CONTRA MEIDIAS,
> A *Literal Translation* of, with Notes, by C. A. M. FENNELL, M.A., late Fellow of Jesus College, cr. 8vo. 2/-

DEMOSTHENES' Three Olynthiac Orations,
> A *Literal Translation* of, 12mo *sewed*, 1/-

DEMOSTHENES LEPTINES,
> Literally Translated by a Graduate, cr. 8vo *sewed*, 2/6

EURIPIDES, ——separate Plays of, Literally Translated, With Notes:—

ALCESTIS, 12mo. *sewed*, 1/-	ION, 12mo. *sewed*, 2/-
ANDROMACHE,12mo *sewed*,1/-	IPHIGENIA IN TAURIS,
BACCHÆ, 12mo. *sewed*, 1/-	12mo. *sewed*, 2/-
HECUBA, 12mo. *sewed*, 1/-	MEDEA, 12mo. *sewed*, 1/-
HERACLIDÆ, 12mo. *sewed*, 1/-	ORESTES, 12mo. *sewed*, 1/-
HERCULES FURENS, 12mo *sewed*, 2/-	PHŒNISSÆ, 12mo. *sewed*, 1/-
	TROADES, 2/-
HIPPOLYTUS, 12mo. *sewed*, 1/-	

SOPHOCLES,——separate Plays of, Literally Translated:—

AJAX, 12mo. *sewed*, 1/-	ŒDIPUS THE KING, 12mo. 1/-
ANTIGONE, 12mo. *sewed*, 1/-	PHILOCTETES, 12mo. *sewed*, 1/-
ELECTRA, 12mo. *sewed*, 1/-	TRACHINIÆ, 12mo. *sewed*, 1/-
ŒDIPUS COLONEUS, 12mo. 1/-	

EURIPIDES HERCULES FURENS,
> Literally Translated, by AUBREY STEWART, M.A., cr. 8vo cloth 2/6

EURIPIDES HERCULES FURENS,
> Parsing of the Principal Words of, 12mo sewed, Sixpence.

EURIPIDIS HIPPOLYTUS,
> With *English Notes*, and a *Literal Translation*, by a Graduate First Class Classical Honours, cr. 8vo 3/6 or interleaved, 4/6

EURIPIDIS MEDEA,
> With *Notes*, and a *Literal Translation*, by W. C. GREEN, M.A., late Fellow of King's College, Assistant Master at Rugby, cr. 8vo interleaved, 5/-

J. HALL & SON'S PUBLICATIONS.

HERODOTUS, Book III.
With *English Notes*, and a *Literal Translation*. 12mo. Interleaved, 4/-

HERODOTUS, Book VI.
With *English notes*, and a *Literal Translation*, by E. S. CROOKE, M. A. late of Pembroke College, cr. 8vo. interleaved, 5/-

HERODOTUS, Book VIII.
With *English Notes*, and a *Literal Translation*, by P. J. F. GANTILLON, M. A. 12mo interleaved, 4/-

HERODOTUS, Book IX.
With *English Notes*, and a *Literal Translation*, by JOHN PERKINS, M. A., Fellow and Tutor of Downing College, Cambridge. Cr. 8vo interleaved, 5/-

HOMER'S ILIAD, Books III & IV.
with *English Notes* and a *Literal Translation*, cr. 8vo interleaved, 5/-

HOMER'S ILIAD, Books XX, XXI, XXII.
with *Eng. Notes*, and a *Lit. Translation*, by E. S. CROOKE, B. A. late of Pembroke College, cr. 8vo interleaved, 5/-

HOMER'S ILIAD, Books XXIII, & XXIV.,
with *English Notes*, and a *Literal Translation*, By E. S. CROOKE, B.A., cr. 8vo. interleaved, 5/-

HOMER'S Iliad, Books I. & II., and Æschylus PROMETHEUS
translated into English Verse, by W. C. GREEN, M.A., late Fellow of King's College. cr. 8vo *sewed*, 3/-

LIVY, Book XXI.
Literally Translated, 12mo 1/6.

LUCANI PHARSALIÆ, LIB. I.
with English Notes and Translation. by J. PERKINS, M. A., Fellow and Tutor of Downing College. cr. 8vo cloth, 5/-

LUCIANI, SOMNIUM (seu vita Luciani), CHARON, PISCATOR, et de LUCTU,
Literally Translated, by W. ARMOUR, Scholar of Magdalene College. cr. 8vo 3/-

PLAUTUS MENAECHMI,
With English Notes, and *Literal Translation*, by AUBREY STEWART, M.A., Fellow of Trinity College. cr. 8vo *interleaved*, 5/-

PLATO'S APOLOGY AND CRITO,
A *New and Literal Translation* of, with Notes, by Rev. W. C. GREEN, M.A., late Fellow of King's College, Assistant Master at Rugby. Cr. 8vo 2/-

QUINTI CURTI RUFI HISTORIARUM ALEXANDRI,
Literally Translated with Marginal Headings. and a life of Alexthe Great, by H. J. C. KNIGHT, B.A., Scholar of S. Catharine's College, cr. 8vo 2/6

SOPHOCLES AJAX;

from the Text of Wunder, with copious *English Explanatory Notes*, &c.; by D. B. HICKIE, LL.D., *Head Master of Hawkshead Grammar School.* 12mo. cloth, 2/6 or interleaved 3/-

TERENCE PHORMIO,

Literally Translated, with Notes, by AUBREY STEWART, M.A., late Fellow of Trinity College, cr. 8vo 3/-

VIRGILII ÆNEIDOS, Lib. III. & IV.

With Critical and Explanatory Notes, and a *New Literal Translation.* By J. PERKINS, M.A., Fellow and Tutor of Downing College. Cr. 8vo cloth, 5/- *interleaved.*

VIRGILII ÆNEIDOS, Lib. V. & VI.

Literally Translated, by E. S. CROOKE, B.A., cr. 8vo 2/-

VIRGILII ÆNEIDOS, Lib. XII.

With English Notes, and a *Literal Translation;* by J. DENMAN, B.C.L., of St John's College, Cambridge. cr. 8vo. interleaved, 4/6

XENOPHON'S ANABASIS, Books I. & II.

Literally Translated, cr. 8vo. 1/6.

XENOPHON'S ANABASIS, Books III. & IV.

From the Text of Bornemann and Dindorf, with *English Notes,* and a *Literal Translation.* By the Rev. EDGAR SANDERSON, M.A., late Scholar of Clare Coll. cr. 8vo interleaved, 5/-

XENOPHON'S ANABASIS, Books VI. & VII.

With *English Notes,* and a *Literal Translation.* cr. 8vo. cloth. interleaved, 5/-

ELEMENTARY HYDROSTATICS:

Its principles explained, illustrated, and applied, by JOHN THURLOW, B. A., Gonville and Caius College, Head Master of Modern Department, Rossall School. cr. 8vo. cloth 2/6

EUCLID,

ENUNCIATIONS and COROLLARIES of the PROPOSITIONS of the FIRST SIX BOOKS together with the ELEVENTH. 18mo sewed, 6d. The same, with Figures, 1/-

A SPECULATION CONCERNING MOLECULAR PHYSICS;

By A. J. STEVENS, M.A., Fellow of St. John's College, 8vo cloth, 1/-

THE CHEMICAL PROCESSES OF THE BRITISH PHARMACOPEIA,

and the Behaviour, with Re-Agents, of their Products, by HENRY J. CHURCH. *Second Edition,* fcp. 8vo. *sewed,* 3/-